The Science Project

by Jesse Leon McCann

Illustrated by Jason Fruchter

SCHOLASTIC INC.

New York   Toronto   London   Auckland   Sydney
Mexico City   New Delhi   Hong Kong   Buenos Aires

Published by Scholastic Inc.,
90 Old Sherman Turnpike, Danbury, CT 06816.

SCHOLASTIC and associated logos are trademarks
and/or registered trademarks of Scholastic Inc.

ISBN 0-439-56271-6

First Scholastic Printing, October 2003

Chapters

"James Isaac Neutron! Did you take the spark plugs from the car again?" Jimmy's mom, Judy, shouted.

"Jumpin' Jupiter, Mom," Jimmy said. "I just remembered that my science project is due today! I need the plugs for my

electro-orbital yo-yo," he added, smiling.

"It's sure to get the best grade in class!"

"How many times do I have to tell you: Auto parts are to stay in the auto!" Jimmy's mom scolded. "Hand them over, mister. You can't break the rules just because you waited until the last moment."

Jimmy gave up the plugs. His robot-dog,
Goddard, thought they smelled mighty tasty.

Jimmy's dad, Hugh, stepped outside as Jimmy ran for the bus. "Boys will be boys!" he tried to explain to his wife. "That is, unless they're men . . . or babies."

Meanwhile, Goddard was helping himself to a spark-plug breakfast.

Chapter 2
Science Is Golden

"Tough luck, Jimmy," Carl said.
"Now you don't have a science
project."

"Not to worry, Carl," Jimmy replied. "I'll present one of my *other* inventions, instead!" He pulled out his super-growth serum and his self-popping popcorn.

"Look at my invention, Jimmy!"
Carl said, when they had reached school.
"It's a nonreturning boomerang!"

Jimmy looked puzzled. "Gee, Carl, that
looks like an ordinary stick."

"That's the way I designed it!" Carl
beamed.

"Hey, Neutron!" someone called. It was
Nick, the most popular boy in school, riding
a skateboard.

"These turbo wheels you invented make my board super kickin'!" Nick said. "Thanks for letting me have them!"

"I said you could *borrow* them," Jimmy pointed out.

"What's *your* science project, Nick?" Carl asked, changing the subject.

"These turbo wheels Jimmy invented," said Nick, as he winked and rode off again.

Jimmy's friend Sheen ran up. "Prepare to be impressed, amazed, and stunned! Taa-daah!"

"Presenting my Ultra Lord Sprout Buddy!"
Sheen exclaimed. "He even grows his own
ultra hair!" Sheen's invention was a clay
statue of Ultra Lord, his favorite superhero,
with grass growing
on its head.

"I'll get an *A*-plus for sure!" Sheen said.

"Me, too!"
said Carl.

"I'm not sure which of my projects to choose. Either could get the highest grade!" Jimmy said confidently.

"Think again, *Nerd*tron!" said a voice that made Jimmy cringe.

It could only be — Cindy Vortex!

SUPER GROWTH SERUM

SELF-POPPING POPCORN

"Miss Fowl will like *my* project best!"
Cindy boasted.

The boys gasped. Cindy was carrying

a box of monsters!

27

"This is my flatworm habitat," Cindy said. "This special lens magnifies the view, making it possible to observe the worms in their habitat—see?" Cindy explained.

Jimmy had to admit, Cindy's project was pretty impressive. But he wouldn't tell her that, of course.

"Cindy's too cool for school, huh, Jimmy?"
said Cindy's best friend, Libby.

"In her own mind," Jimmy said, smirking.

But Jimmy was worried. What if Miss Fowl liked Cindy's project best? He wasn't really sure *either* of his inventions could get the best grade!

"I've got to guarantee that I get the best grade," Jimmy thought. "Cindy *Snore*tex won't beat me!"

Chapter 4
Spills and Pops

"All right, class, from this point on, no tinkering with any of the projects," their teacher, Miss Fowl, began. "This class has been known to have . . . uh . . . mishaps . . . from students trying to outdo each other!"

Suddenly Jimmy had an idea. "I know! I'll secretly add a little super-growth serum to my popcorn! It's sneaky, but I'll beat Cindy for sure!"

Meanwhile, Carl was called to the front of the class to do his presentation. "For years," he began, "Australians have been throwing crooked sticks and hitting themselves on the head . . ."

Cindy eyed Jimmy. "No fair, Neutron!" she whispered angrily. "You heard Miss Fowl. It's too late to make changes!"

" . . . sometimes giving themselves huge, ugly lumps," Carl continued.

Jimmy ignored Cindy and began to
pour a few drops of the growth serum on
the popcorn kernels.

Just then Cindy yanked on Jimmy's shirt.
Jimmy's super-growth serum spilled all
over his popcorn and onto the floor!

The popcorn kernels started growing . . . and **growing** . . . and **growing!**

Chapter 5
Avalanche!

Beach ball–sized popcorn exploded around
the classroom! Cindy jumped back, landed
on Nick's turbo-skateboard, and went flying!

She slammed into Carl, which caused the nonreturning boomerang to fly out of his hand!

The stick hit Cindy's flatworm habitat,
which broke into a thousand pieces!

Jimmy dove to catch the flatworms,
but he wasn't fast enough. To his horror, the
little worms landed in the puddle of
super-growth serum!

The flatworms started growing bigger.

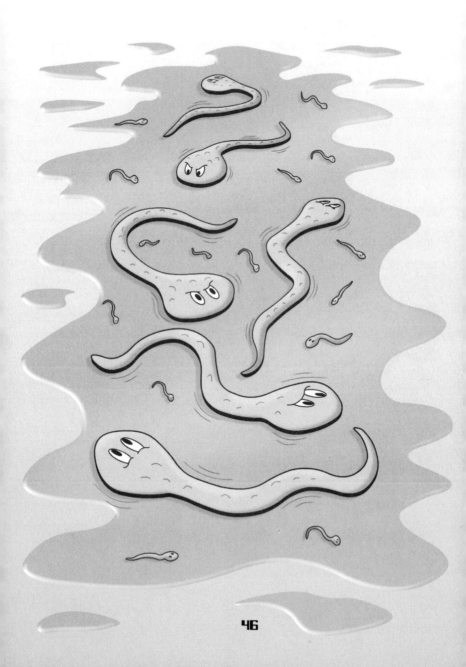

And **bigger**.

And bigger!

Soon the worms were as big as cars!

Before long, the giant flatworms swarmed through the school, knocking holes in the floors and ceilings.

An avalanche of popcorn trapped Jimmy
and Libby!

Chapter 6
Mom and Dad
to the Rescue

"If only Cindy hadn't made me spill my super-growth serum!" Jimmy's mind was racing. He had to do something! Then . . . "Brain Blast!" he exclaimed.

"Libby, can I use your cell phone?" he asked.

"If you can reach it!" Libby grunted. "Plus pay any roaming fees."

Jimmy snagged Libby's phone and dialed. "Hi, Mom!" he said. "Oh, everything's swell. Can you do me a favor?"

Jimmy then asked his parents to bring his super-shrinking serum to school.

But the car wouldn't start!

Burp!

"Goddard, did you eat those spark plugs?" demanded Judy.

"Burp!" the robot-dog replied.

Jimmy's parents thought quickly. "Where there's a will, there's a way," puffed Hugh. "That is . . . unless it's a boy named Will. Or a man . . . or baby."

Jimmy's parents arrived just in time.
They shrunk the worms down to normal
size. Jimmy and Libby were rescued. The
school was saved!

While the school was being repaired,
Miss Fowl gathered her class on the lawn.
Since the Ultra Lord Sprout Buddy was the
only project that survived, Sheen got
the highest grade.

A++

"Pukin' Pluto!" Jimmy sighed.

"James Isaac Neutron," Jimmy's mom whispered, "don't you have something to say to the class?"

Jimmy nodded shyly. "This whole thing is my fault," he admitted. "I shouldn't have broken the rules just to win. I'm sorry."

Later, the Neutrons were back home, safe and sound.

"Jim, Jimmy, James, Jimbo," said Hugh. "You've learned a valuable lesson today."

"You bet, Dad," Jimmy agreed. "No more breaking the rules. And I'm starting my next project today. After all," he said wisely, "it's the early bird who catches the worm!"